토끼의 심판

The Rabbit's Judgment

Suzanne Crowder Han  Illustrated by Yumi Heo

Henry Holt and Company
New York

Henry Holt and Company, Inc. / *Publishers since 1866* / 115 West 18th Street / New York, New York 10011
Henry Holt is a registered trademark of Henry Holt and Company, Inc.
Text copyright © 1991 by Suzanne Crowder Han / Illustrations copyright © 1994 by Yumi Heo
Published in Canada by Fitzhenry & Whiteside Ltd., 195 Allstate Parkway, Markham, Ontario L3R 4T8.

"The Rabbit's Judgment" originally appeared, in slightly different form,
in *Korean Folk and Fairy Tales* © 1991 by Suzanne Crowder Han,
published by Hollym Corporation; Publishers, Seoul, Korea.

Library of Congress Cataloging-in-Publication Data
Han, Suzanne Crowder.
The rabbit's judgment / Suzanne Crowder Han; illustrated by Yumi Heo.
English and Korean.
Summary: Tricked into freeing a hungry tiger from a trap, a man refuses to let the
tiger eat him until they get another opinion on the situation from a disinterested party.
[1. Folklore — Korea.   2. Korean language materials — Bilingual.]   I. Heo, Yumi, ill.   II. Title.
PZ50.563.H3   1994   398.21 — dc20   [E]   93-11031

ISBN 0-8050-2674-6
First Edition — 1994

Printed in the United States of America on acid-free paper. ∞
1   3   5   7   9   10   8   6   4   2

Note on the Korean alphabet

Han-gul, the Korean alphabet, did not evolve; it was purposefully invented by a group of scholars under the direction of King Sejong, who promulgated it in 1446. Until that time, Koreans used Chinese characters for writing because, even though they had a spoken language, they had no written language of their own.

Han-gul is phonetic and syllabic, comprising ten vowels and fourteen consonants. The shape of each vowel and consonant derives from the configuration of the mouth, tongue, and throat during the articulation of that sound. Writing may be done horizontally from left to right, or vertically from right to left, which is the traditional way of writing Korean.

For my daughter, Minsu

—S. C. H.

For my mother and father

—Y. H.

Author's note

Like its once mountainous landscape, Korea's folktales are populated with a wide array of animals and insects, and the most prevalent are the rabbit and the tiger. The rabbit is always portrayed as clever and witty, but the tiger is characterized in different ways. In some stories, he is weak, stupid, conniving, and ungrateful; in others, he is noble, magnanimous, powerful, and godlike.

The Rabbit's Judgment is taken from my book *Korean Folk and Fairy Tales*, a collection of sixty-four Korean tales. I read many Korean- and English-language collections to study and compare the retelling styles, the structures of the stories, and the depictions of the characters. Versions of this particular tale vary. In *Folk Tales from Korea* by Zong In-sob, the story has only three characters: a man, a tiger, and a toad; a version from Yi Ka-won's *Han-guk horang-i iyagi (Korean Tiger Tales)* has the man asking a pine tree and a crow for their judgments, and the tiger being tricked by a fox at the end. In other retellings, the tiger is the title character. Most versions of this particular story, however, included three plants and animals being asked to pass judgment, and a rabbit finally tricking the tiger. In my retelling of "The Rabbit's Judgment," I drew upon the way the rabbit and the tiger were depicted in numerous stories to make the characters colorful and accessible to the reader.

—S.C.H.

옛날 옛적에, 동물과 나무들이 서로 얘기를 하며 살았을 적에 호랑이
한 마리가 먹이를 찾아 숲속을 어슬렁거리다가 그만 깊은 구덩이에 빠졌
습니다. 호랑이는 그 구덩이를 빠져 나오려고 몇번이고 애를 썼지만 너무
가파르고 깊어서 기어오를 수도 뛰어오를 수도 없었습니다. 도와달라고 외
쳐보기도 했지만 아무도 오지 않았습니다.

LONG, LONG AGO, when plants and animals talked, a tiger fell into
a deep pit while roaming through the forest in search of food. He
tried over and over to get out but the walls were too steep for him
to climb and he could not jump high enough to reach the opening.
He called for help but none came.

그 다음날 아침에도 호랑이는 목이 쉬도록 도움을 청했습니다. 이제 구덩이 안에서 죽을 수 밖에 없는 운명이라고 생각하며 배고프고 지친 호랑이는 땅바닥에 쓰러졌습니다. 바로 그 때 발자국 소리가 들렸습니다.

The next morning he called for help until he was hoarse. Hungry and exhausted, he slumped down on the ground, thinking that he was doomed to die in the pit. But then he heard footsteps.

"살려주세요! 살려주세요!" 호랑이는 큰 소리로 외쳤습니다.
"저런, 호랑이구나!" 한 나그네가 구덩이를 내려다 보면서 말했습니다.
"제발, 제발 저를 여기서 꺼내주세요!" 호랑이는 사정하였습니다. "저를 도와만 주신다면 평생동안 그 은혜를 잊지 않겠습니다."

"Help! Help!" he cried desperately.
"Oh! A tiger!" said a man, peering over the side of the pit.
"Please! Please help me out of here!" pleaded the tiger.
"If you help me, I won't forget you as long as I live."

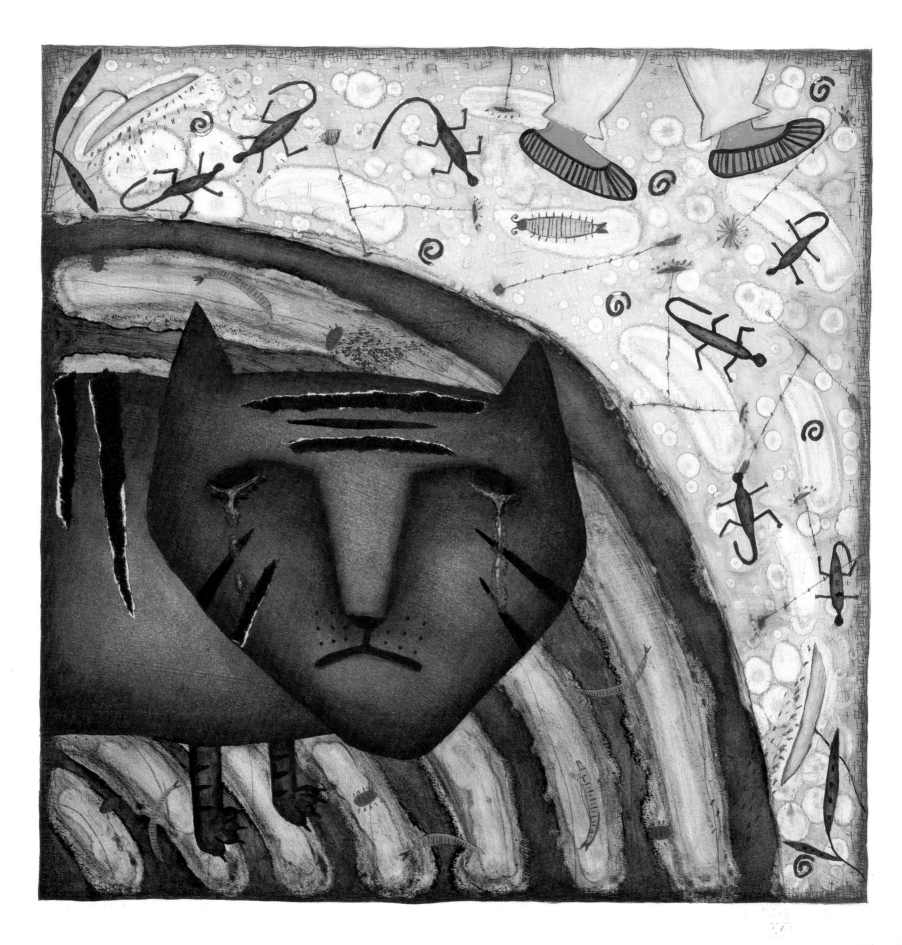

나그네는 호랑이를 딱하게 생각했지만 잡아먹힐까봐 무서웠습니다. "도와주고는 싶지만 다음일이 걱정이 되어 부득이 거절할 수 밖에 없네. 나를 용서하게나. 나는 가야겠네." 나그네는 이렇게 말하고 가던 길로 향했습니다.

"천만에요. 절대로 그럴리가 없습니다. 제발 그렇게 생각하지 마시고 저를 살려주십시오!" 호랑이가 외쳤습니다. "걱정하지 마세요! 맹세합니다! 절대로 해치지 않겠습니다! 제발 저를 여기서 꺼내주세요! 제발 부탁합니다! 이렇게 애원합니다! 저를 여기서 꺼내주신다면 평생동안 그 은혜를 잊지 않겠습니다. 제발 저를 살려주세요!"

The man felt sorry for the tiger but he was afraid of being eaten. "I would like to help you but, I'm sorry, the thought of what might happen makes me refuse. Please forgive me. I must be on my way," said the man and he began walking down the path.

"No! No! Please don't think like that! Please help me!" cried the tiger. "You don't have to worry, I promise. I won't hurt you. Please help me out. Please! I beg you! If you get me out, I'll be forever grateful to you. Please!"

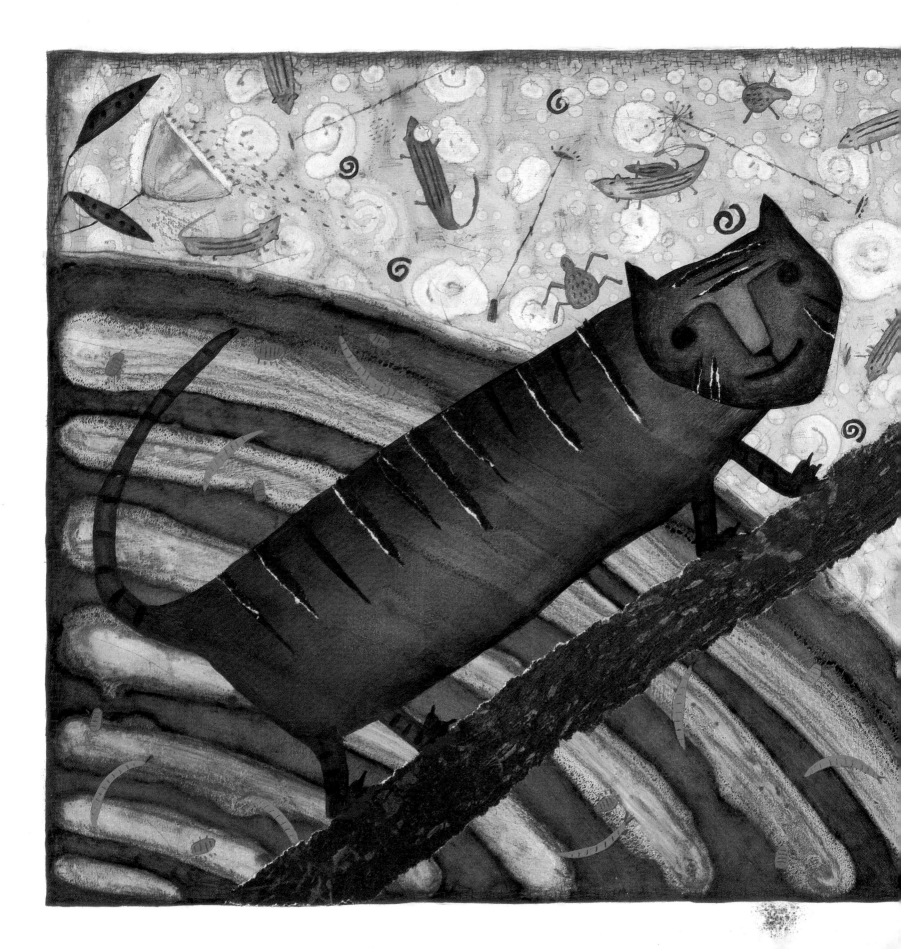

호랑이의 외치는 소리 하도 측
은하게 들려서 나그네는 발걸음을
돌려 구덩이로 되돌아 갔습니다.
나그네는 근처에서 큰 통나무 하
나를 찾아 냈습니다. "자, 이 통
나무를 타고 올라오게." 나그네는
통나무를 구덩이 안으로 내려 놓
으며 말했습니다.

The tiger sounded so pitiful
that the man turned around
and walked back to the pit. He
looked around until he found a
big log. "Here, climb up this,"
he said, lowering the log into
the pit.

호랑이는 통나무를 타고 올라와 나그네와 얼굴을 마주 대하고 바라 보았습니다. 호랑이는 군침을 흘리며 나그네 주위를 맴돌기 시작했습니다.

"아니 ! 나를 해치지 않겠다고 약속하지 않았나? 이것이 친절에 보답하는 길인가?"

"배가 고파 죽을 지경인데 약속 따위가 무슨 소용이람 ! 며칠째 아무것도 못 먹었는데 말이야."

The tiger climbed up the log and came face to face with the man. His mouth watered and he began circling him.

"Hey! Wait a minute! Didn't you promise not to hurt me? Is this your idea of gratefulness? Is this how you repay a kindness?"

"What do I care about a promise when I'm starving! I haven't eaten for days!"

"잠깐! 잠깐!" 나그네가 외쳤습니다. "당신이 나를 잡아 먹는 것이 과연 옳은 일인지 저기 있는 저 소나무에게 물어봅시다."

"좋아!" 호랑이가 말했습니다. "그렇지만 잡아 먹을거야. 배가 몹시 고프다구."

나그네와 호랑이는 소나무에게 앞뒤 사정을 설명하였습니다.

"Wait! Wait!" cried the man. "Let's ask that pine tree if it is right for you to eat me."

"All right," said the tiger. "But I'm awfully hungry."

The tiger and the man explained the situation to the pine tree.

"인간은 도대체 은혜에 대해 말할 자격이 없어." 소나무가 말했습니다. "당신네 인간들은 우리 나무의 잎과 가지를 쳐 땔감으로 쓰지. 게다가 우리가 크게 자라려면 몇 년이나 걸리는데, 겨우 겨우 자라나면 당신네들이 우리를 이리저리 마구 잘라서 집이니 장롱따위로 만들어버리지. 더군다나 저기 있는 구덩이를 판 것도 인간이라구. 은혜? 웃기는군! 호랑이님은 배고픔이나 달래시지요!"

"What do men know about gratefulness?" said the pine tree. "Why, your kind take our leaves and limbs to make fires to heat your homes and cook your food. And it takes us years to grow big but when we finally do, you cut us down and cut us up to make timber and planks for houses and furniture and the like. Moreover, it was a man that dug that pit. Gratefulness, indeed! Don't give it another thought, Tiger. You just go ahead and satisfy your hunger!"

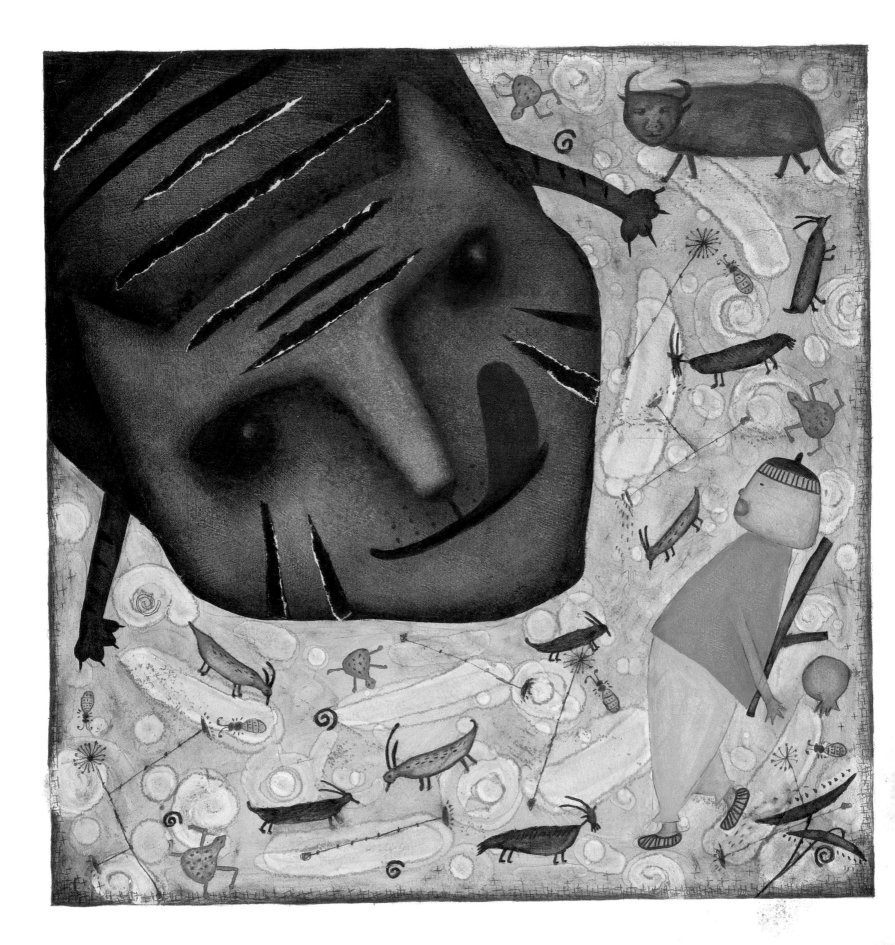

"자, 어떻게 생각하나, 나그네 양반?" 호랑이는 입맛을 쩝쩝 다시며 슬금슬금 나그네에게 다가갔습니다.

바로 그 때 소 한 마리가 어슬렁어슬렁 다가왔습니다. "잠깐만요!" 나그네가 외쳤습니다. "저 소에게 심판을 부탁해봅시다."

"Now what do you think of that?" asked the tiger, smacking his lips loudly and slinking toward the man.

Just at that moment an ox wandered by. "Wait! Wait!" cried the man. "Let's ask that ox to judge."

호랑이도 그러자고했습니다. 그들은 소에게 지금까지의 일을 자세히 설명한 뒤 의견을 구했습니다.

"그거야 나라면 생각하고 말고 할 것도 없어요." 호랑이 쪽으로 돌아서며 소가 말했습니다. "잡아 먹으세요 !"

The tiger agreed, so they explained everything to the ox and asked his opinion.

"Well, as far as I'm concerned, there's no question about what to do," said the ox, turning to the tiger. "You should eat him up!"

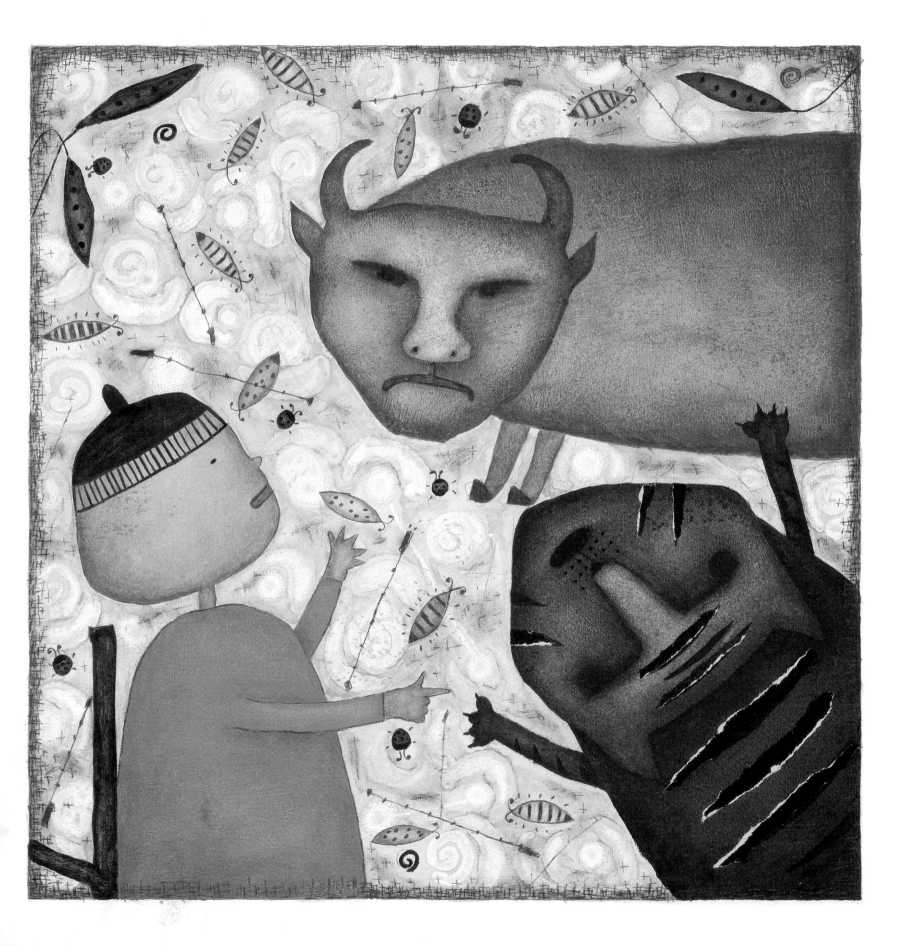

"호랑이님도 아시다시피 우리
소들은 태어나서 부터 내내 인간
들을 위해 부지런히 일을 하지요.
등에 무거운 짐을 실어 나르기도
하고 인간들이 농사를 지으라고
논밭을 갈기도 하지요. 그런데도
우리가 늙으면 어떻게 하는지 아
세요? 우리를 죽여서 고기를 먹
고, 가죽으로는 여러가지 물건을
만들어 쓴답니다. 그러니 제게는
저 나그네에게 고마움을 느껴야
한다느니 따위의 얘기는 하지 마
세요. 그냥 잡아 잡수시라구요!"

"You see, from the time we're
born we oxen work diligently
for men. We carry heavy loads
on our backs and plow up the
ground so they can grow food.
But what do they do when
we're old? They kill us and eat
our flesh and use our hides to
make all kinds of things. So
don't talk to me about being
grateful to him. Just eat him!"

"어때? 모두들 찬성하지않나. 이제 죽을 준비나 하시지." 호랑이가 금방이라도 덮칠듯이 말했습니다.

나그네는 이제 꼼짝없이 죽었구나 하고 생각했습니다. 바로 그 때 토끼 한 마리가 깡총 깡총 다가왔습니다.

"호랑이님, 잠깐만 기다려 주세요!" 나그네가 사정했습니다.

"또 뭐야?" 호랑이가 으르렁댔습니다.

"제발 마지막으로 한번만 더 기회를 주십시오." 나그네가 애걸했습니다. "저기 저 토끼에게 과연 내가 잡아먹혀야 되는지 심판을 해주도록 부탁합시다."

"무슨 소용이 있을라구? 똑같은 답이 나올게 뻔한데."

"제발 한번만 더 봐주십시오." 나그네가 애걸복걸하였습니다.

"좋아, 그렇지만 이번이 마지막이야. 배가 고파 죽겠단 말이야 !"

"See! Everyone agrees. Now get ready to die," said the tiger, crouching to pounce.

The man thought that it must surely be his time to die. But then a rabbit came hopping by.

"Wait, Tiger! Wait!" shouted the man.

"Now what?" roared the tiger.

"Please give me one last chance," begged the man. "Let's ask that rabbit to judge whether I should be eaten or not."

"Oh, what's the use? You know the answer will be the same."

"Please, please," pleaded the man.

"Oh, all right. But this is the last time. I'm starving!"

호랑이와 나그네는 토끼에게 그들의 사정을 이야기하였습니다. 토끼는 매우 주의 깊게 이야기를 들었습니다. 이야기를 들은 다음 눈을 감고 그 큰 귀를 쓰다듬었습니다. 조금 후에 토끼는 눈을 뜨더니 천천히 뜸을 들이며 말했습니다. "두 분께서 방금 하신 말씀은 잘 알겠습니다. 그러나 현명한 심판을 위해 저쪽 구덩이가 있는 곳에 가서 다시 한번 얘기해주십시오. 자 가시지요."

So the tiger and the man told the rabbit their story. The rabbit listened carefully. Then he closed his eyes and stroked one of his long ears. After a few seconds he opened his eyes and spoke slowly and deliberately. "I well understand what the two of you have said. But if I am to make a wise judgment we should go to that pit and you should tell me again what happened. So lead the way."

호랑이와 나그네는 토끼를 구덩이로 데려갔습니다.
"구덩이가 정말 깊군요." 구덩이를 내려다 보며 토끼가 말했습니다. "그러니까 호랑이 당신은 저 아래에 있었고, 나그네께서는 여기 이렇게 서 계셨다는 말씀이지요?" 호랑이와 나그네에게 토끼가 물었습니다.
"자, 그럼 그때 그대로 자리를 잡아보시지요. 그러면 제가 심판을 내릴 수 있겠습니다."
호랑이는 아무 생각도 없이 구덩이 속으로 뛰어내렸습니다. 호랑이는 배가 매우 고팠으므로 빨리 심판을 끝내고 나그네를 잡아먹을 생각만 했던 것입니다. 나그네는 구덩이 가장자리에서 아래를 내려다 보았습니다.

The tiger and the man led the rabbit the few short steps to the pit.
"Well, it certainly is deep," said the rabbit, looking down into the pit. "Let's see, you say you were down there, and you were standing here like this?" he said to the tiger and then to the man. "Well, if you get in those positions, then I can make a judgment."
Without giving it a second thought, the hungry tiger jumped down into the pit. The man peered over the edge.

"그래 두분께서 그렇게 계셨단 말씀이지요?" 토끼가 말했습니다. "자, 이제야 심판을 내릴 수가 있겠습니다. 이 나그네가 저 호랑이를 구덩이로 부터 구해주므로써 문제가 시작되었군. 다시 말해서 이 나그네 양반이 친절을 베풀지 않고 호랑이를 저 구덩이에 내버려 두었으면 문제가 전혀 생기지 않았을거란 말이야. 그러니 내 생각에는 나그네는 그냥 자기 갈 길을 가고 호랑이는 그대로 구덩이 속에 남아 있으면 되겠군.

"자, 그럼 두 분 다 안녕." 영리한 토끼는 이렇게 말하고 깡총깡총 뛰어갔습니다.

"So, that is how the two of you were," said the rabbit. "Now I can judge. The problem started when this man helped that tiger out of this pit. In other words, if the man had not shown any kindness and had left the tiger in the pit, there wouldn't be a problem. So I think the man should continue his journey and the tiger should remain in the pit.

"Now, a good day to the both of you," said the clever rabbit and he hopped away.

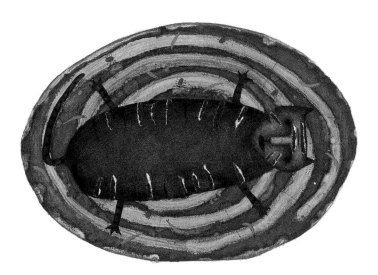